Sophie

TAKES
TO THE

Sky

Sophie

TAKES TO THE

Sky

KATHERINE WOODFINE

With illustrations by
BRIONY MAY SMITH

Kane Miller
A DIVISION OF EDC PUBLISHING

First American Edition 2020
Kane Miller, A Division of EDC Publishing

First published in 2019 in Great Britain
by Barrington Stoke Ltd
Text © 2019 Katherine Woodfine
Illustrations © 2019 Briony May Smith
The moral rights of the author and illustrator have been asserted.

For information contact:
Kane Miller, A Division of EDC Publishing
P.O. Box 470663
Tulsa, OK 74147-0663
www.kanemiller.com
www.edcpub.com
www.usbornebooksandmore.com

Library of Congress Control Number: 2019940413

Manufactured by Regent Publishing Services, Hong Kong
Printed November 2019 in ShenZhen, Guangdong, China
1 2 3 4 5 6 7 8 9 10
ISBN: 978-1-68464-029-4

For O.D.

Contents

Chapter 1

Scaredy-Cat Sophie

A long time ago, in a small French village by the sea, there lived a little girl called Sophie.

Sophie lived with her mama and her older sister Flora in a white house with green shutters, not far from the village square.

In the village, everyone knew everything about everybody else. And the most important thing that they all knew about Sophie was that she was scared of *everything*.

Sophie was scared of mice and spiders. She was scared of thunderstorms and shadows.

She was scared of the big black cat that belonged to Annette next door and the big brown dog that barked outside Pierre's farm.

She was scared of the ghost that might live in the cupboard in her bedroom and the monster that might hide under her bed.

Sophie shivered when she went down to the cellar in the dark. She shook when she rode in a carriage. She screamed when she heard a loud noise.

"Oh, Sophie!" said Mama. "What are we going to do with you?"

When Sophie was scared, Mama was kind and comforting. But Flora was not kind at all. Flora was brave and bold, and she thought Sophie's fears were silly.

She had a name she called Sophie in secret, when Mama could not hear her: *Scaredy-cat Sophie.*

Sophie hated the nickname. She wished she wasn't always frightened, but she just couldn't help it.

It was no good. She was going to be *Scaredy-cat Sophie* forever.

Chapter 2

The Fair is Coming!

One day, when Flora was playing with her friends, she found out something very exciting. A fair was coming to the nearby town and everyone was talking about it.

A big poster had been put up in the village square. Flora and her best friends Felix and Julie read about the fair and all the wonderful things they would see.

"There'll be clowns and conjurers and dancers and acrobats!" cried Felix.

"There'll be elephants and tigers and musicians and jugglers!" cried Julie.

COME TO THE FAIR!

"There'll be a firework display
and a whirligig wheel and all kinds of
delicious things to eat!" cried Flora.

Everyone agreed that the fair would
be thrilling. But the most thrilling thing
of all was the balloonist.

Chapter 3

Balloon Madness

Even in the little village where Sophie lived, everyone had heard about the new hot-air balloons and the brave men who flew them.

They knew all about the balloon flight at the royal palace.

Two clever balloonists had sent a
sheep, a duck and a cockerel up into
the sky in a beautiful blue balloon.
And the king and queen of France had
watched it. Just think of that!

Now more and more balloonists were traveling high up into the air in their marvelous balloons. One of them had flown right over the city of Paris. Another had flown all the way across the sea to England!

Balloon madness was sweeping across France. There were drawings of the balloons in the newspapers. There were poems and songs about the balloonists and their amazing adventures. Grand ladies painted designs of balloons on their fans. They wore dresses with enormous puffed sleeves in the shape of the hot-air balloons. People bought balloon plates and balloon cups, balloon clocks and balloon lamps, balloon hats and balloon hair ribbons.

Everyone wanted to see the balloonists as they flew high above France. Now the people of Sophie's village would have their chance.

Everyone stared at the picture of the balloonist on the poster in the village square.

"Isn't he handsome?" said Annette.

"I wonder if I should do *my* hair like that?" said Pierre.

"It will be wonderful to see a real-life adventurer!" cried Flora.

Sophie stared too. She liked the look of the balloonist — but what she liked even more was the picture of the

hot-air balloon as it sailed across the
wide blue sky.

Chapter 4

Left at Home

Mama promised that she would take Flora, Julie and Felix to the fair to see the balloon flight. "But what about Sophie?" she asked.

"Oh, *she* won't want to come to the fair!" Flora said. "She'd be far too frightened! It will be too loud and too crowded."

"Well, actually—" began Sophie.

"She'd be scared of fireworks! She'd be terrified of tigers and elephants! *She* wouldn't want to see a hot-air balloon. She'd probably scream. Or cry."

"But maybe—" Sophie tried again.

"Anyway, we'll go to town in the carriage," said Flora. "Sophie doesn't like carriages. She gets frightened."

Sophie fell silent. It was true that she hated riding in the carriage. The horses were so big and the carriage was so loud and bumpy, and what if there was an accident on the road? It made her feel sick just thinking about it.

Flora was right. Scaredy-cat Sophie couldn't go to the fair — and that was that.

Chapter 5

The Black Cat

Soon, the great day of the fair arrived. Mama, Flora, Julie and Felix set off to town, while Sophie was left at home.

Before she went, Mama set out some food for Sophie's dinner — some bread, some cheese and two ripe peaches. "Are you sure you will be all right by yourself?" she asked.

"Of course I will," said Sophie.

But just the same, Sophie did not feel very happy as she watched Flora skip off with her friends toward the village square where they would get the carriage to town.

To cheer herself up, she went into the garden. She lay down in the grass and watched the butterflies and bees buzzing in the flowers. She stared up into the blue sky. What would it be like to see a bright balloon floating across it? How magical it would be! If only she could see it for herself ...

Just then, she heard a noise in the bushes. Annette's big black cat had come into their garden. It was walking straight toward Sophie with its long black tail in the air.

Sophie shivered and jumped up in fear. But the cat did not bite or scratch. Instead it kept walking toward her and then wound itself around her ankles in a very friendly way.

Sophie reached out a hand and stroked the cat. Its fur felt warm and very soft. Soon it began to purr — a rich, deep, happy sound.

Sophie was amazed. As she stroked the cat, a thought flew suddenly into her mind. If she could be brave enough to overcome her fear of the big black cat, then maybe — just maybe — she could be brave enough to go to the fair after all!

She stared up into the sky again
and thought of the marvelous balloon.
She knew she would never be as brave
as the balloonist, sailing through the
clouds, but perhaps she could be brave
enough to see him flying for herself.

Chapter 6

The Brown Dog

Sophie went back inside the house and put on her best dress. She wrapped up the bread, cheese and peaches in a clean cloth.

Outside, the cat was still sitting in the garden, washing its face with its paw.

"Wish me luck, black cat," Sophie whispered. "I'm going to the fair!"

The cat meowed as if it knew exactly what she had said.

Sophie knew it would be too late to catch up with Mama and Flora. Their carriage had already left. But the town was only three miles away. She thought she could walk there in time to see the balloon flight.

She set out along the road that led to town. But before she had left the village, she stopped in her tracks. She could hear the loud and terrible sound of a dog barking.

It was Pierre's dog — the big brown one.

"Woof! *Woof! WOOF!*" it barked, as if to say, "Stay away!"

Sophie knew she would have to pass the farm on her way to the town and at once she began to shiver and shake. What if the big dog rushed out and jumped at her? What if it growled and chased her? What if it bit her with its sharp teeth?

Suddenly, going to the fair all by herself seemed impossible. Should she give up and run back home, where she would be safe?

But then she remembered the black cat, which had not hissed or scratched. Trying to be brave, Sophie crept slowly forward.

As she came closer to the farm, her heart began to bump. The dog was barking louder and louder, and soon her hands began to tremble.

Then, all at once, the enormous dog bounded toward her — and Sophie screamed!

But the dog did not growl or bite. It was not fierce at all; it was friendly and excited. It wagged its tail and bounced around her. "Woof! *Woof! WOOF!*" it barked, as if to say, "Come and play with me!"

Pierre came rushing into the yard. "Get down!" he called. "You silly dog! You'll frighten Sophie!"

"I'm not frightened," said Sophie —
and it was true. She gave the dog's
shaggy fur a soft pat and he licked her
hand.

"Looks like you've made friends," said Pierre in surprise. "Where are you off to this morning? The beach?"

"I'm going to town, to see the fair," Sophie answered.

Pierre looked even more surprised, but all he said was, "Actually, I'm going to town too. Would you like to ride with me in my cart?"

Sophie thought about how much she hated the loud, bumpy carriage. She looked at Pierre's old cart. His enormous cart horse was much bigger and more frightening than the carriage horses. The thought of riding in the cart made her feel sick — but she really wanted to see that wonderful hot-air balloon.

"Yes, please, I'd like to ride to the fair with you," she said.

Chapter 7

All the Fun of the Fair

Sophie soon found that riding in Pierre's cart was much nicer than the bumpy carriage. The big cart horse plodded so slowly down the long lanes that she did not need to worry about accidents. Now and then a carriage rushed past them or a horseman galloped by, but most of the time their journey was peaceful.

After a while, Sophie began to feel hungry and took out her dinner. Pierre had brought his dinner with him too — some bread, some ham and some sweet red cherries. They shared the food and Sophie fed a piece of ham to the brown dog.

As they came closer to the town, the road grew busy. Soon they could see the fair in the distance. Sophie saw colorful tents, smelled smoke and heard the sound of music.

Pierre stopped the cart close to the entrance. "I'll leave you here," he said.

"Aren't you coming to the fair?" asked Sophie. She started to feel nervous again.

"I've got to go to the market first," said Pierre. "But I'll come to the fair later. Perhaps I'll see you there?"

Sophie stared at the crowds of people. She felt very nervous, but she remembered to say thank you as she climbed down from the cart.

"Wish me luck, brown dog!" she whispered as she patted him goodbye — and then Pierre went on his way.

All alone now, Sophie looked
around her.

The fair was enormous. There was
so much to see: stalls selling cakes
and roasted nuts; big posters showing
fire-eaters and firework displays;
and signs pointing to the "Wonderful
Whirligig Wheel." The air was full of
delicious smells of spices, caramel and
chocolate.

Nearby, a musician was playing a jolly tune on a violin. Another played an accordion and a third beat time on a drum. "Come and dance with us!" they called out to Sophie.

"See my Marvelous Magic Show!" cried a conjurer from outside a striped tent.

"Cross my palm with silver and find out your fortune!" called a fortune-teller from behind a curtain that glittered with stars.

But Sophie did not want to do any of these things. She knew exactly what she was here to see and that was the wonderful hot-air balloon.

Chapter 8

A Surprising Adventure

It was not difficult for Sophie to find what she was looking for. The balloon was enormous — much bigger and taller than anything else. Crowds of people stood looking at the magnificent balloon, but the famous balloonist was nowhere to be seen.

Sophie crept closer. She stared at the balloon that would soon be high up in the sky. She gazed at the beautiful blue silk and the brightly colored flags that hung all around it. She saw that there was a big basket underneath the balloon for the balloonist to ride in. Strong ropes tied the basket to the balloon.

Sophie put out a hand to touch the basket. Just fancy that — she had touched the wonderful balloon! But it would be even better if she was brave enough to slip *inside* the basket. Then she'd be able to tell Flora that Scaredy-cat Sophie had climbed into the very balloon that would soon travel up into the sky!

Before that moment, Sophie would never have thought of doing anything so bold. She'd have been far too worried that she might get in trouble. But now she thought of the black cat and the brown dog, and she decided it was time to have an adventure.

She picked up the skirts of her best dress and got quickly into the balloon's basket before anyone saw her.

There, she thought. *Just wait until Flora hears that I've been inside the marvelous balloon!*

She was about to climb out again when she heard loud voices and a burst of music.

The famous balloonist had arrived and the crowd was cheering and clapping. Sophie dived quickly behind some sacks. She peeped out to see the balloonist climbing into the basket. He was beautifully dressed and just as handsome as on the poster.

"Behold my wonderful balloon!" he called to the crowd. "Witness the wonder of flight!"

Sophie felt the balloon give a sudden lurch. She saw that the balloonist had untied the ropes that kept the balloon fixed to the ground.

All at once, the hot-air balloon began to rise up into the air!

Chapter 9

Sophie Flies High

The balloon rose higher and higher and swung from side to side. Sophie was so frightened that she didn't know what to do. She'd never been so scared in her life. Not mice, nor spiders, nor thunderstorms, nor even monsters under the bed could ever be as terrifying as this.

The balloon gave another lurch. Her heart pounded and she trembled all over. It was all she could do not to scream out loud.

But after a moment or two, the wild noise of the crowds and the music began to fade away. Soon, all Sophie could hear was the sound of wind in her ears. The balloon was no longer lurching to and fro — instead, it was lifting smoothly and steadily. Everything was still and peaceful.

She peeped out from her hiding place and saw that they were high up in the air, floating through the sky. It was so beautiful that, all at once, she forgot to be frightened.

She had never known anywhere so perfectly quiet and calm. She felt light, as though she had left all her fears and worries on the ground behind her.

"It's *wonderful* ..." she whispered aloud.

"Argh!" shrieked the balloonist in alarm. "W-who are you? What are you doing here?"

"I didn't mean to scare you!" said Sophie, her cheeks pink. "I got into your balloon to have a look at it and then you took off before I had time to get out again. I'm very sorry!"

The balloonist stared at her. He looked pale and sweaty. "You almost frightened me to death!" he exclaimed, and patted his brow with a large spotty silk handkerchief. "My goodness! I think you are the first little girl ever to fly in a hot-air balloon. How brave and bold you must be!"

It was Sophie's turn to stare now. *Her* — Scaredy-cat Sophie — brave and bold?

"Well, since you're here and you can't get out now, you'd better make the most of your balloon ride," said the balloonist. "Come over here and look!"

Sophie came and stood beside him. She could see the whole of the fair spread out beneath them — the colored tents, the stalls, the big whirligig wheel and all the people gazing up at the balloon.

She could see a tall figure that might be Mama, and at her side a smaller figure that could be Flora.

And could that be Pierre, with his brown dog beside him? She waved her hand to them all, even though she knew they would never be able to see her from so far away.

The balloon rose up, still higher. Sophie stared at the people growing smaller and smaller — and then she stared out at the wide, wonderful blue sky.

Together she and the balloonist stood in silence as they enjoyed the stillness and the wind on their faces while the balloon climbed up and up toward the clouds.

Chapter 10

Blue-Sky Dreams

Sophie could have stayed up in the sky for a long, long time. But at last her new friend said their flight had to come to an end and he piloted the balloon slowly down to a field very close to the fair.

It felt strange to be back on the ground with grass beneath her feet.

"Better not tell anyone that you went up in the balloon," said the balloonist. "If they found out, they'd all want a turn! And, er ... if you don't mind, I'd rather you didn't say anything about me screaming like that," he added, looking red in the face. "It wouldn't be very good for my image if people knew that I'd been so scared of a little girl!"

Sophie nodded. She knew all about being scared. And she didn't mind keeping her amazing balloon adventure a secret. Somehow that made it even more special.

She thanked the balloonist and said goodbye, and then hurried back toward the fair. It was as crowded and noisy as ever, but she walked lightly now. It felt as if she was skipping through the clouds.

Before long, she saw Flora and her friends. They were eating lollipops and cakes. "*Sophie!*" yelled Flora. "What are *you* doing here?"

"Pierre told us you'd come, but we didn't believe him!" said Julie, her eyes round.

"Weren't you scared, coming to the fair all by yourself?" asked Felix.

"Well, I was a bit," said Sophie. "But I thought it would be an adventure!"

"Did you see the balloon flight? Wasn't it incredible? Wasn't the balloonist *brave*?" asked Flora.

Sophie could see the balloonist in the distance. He had excited fans all around him and they were telling him how brave he was.

He saw Sophie looking at him and gave her a quick wink.

"Oh yes, I saw the balloon," she said. "It was wonderful. But now I'm going for a ride on the whirligig wheel. Who wants to come with me?"

"I do!" all three of them shouted.

Mama and Pierre watched and waved from the ground as the whirligig wheel carried them high into the air. The others screamed, but for once Sophie didn't feel even the smallest bit scared. Being up high made her remember how it had felt to float through the air in the marvelous blue balloon.

She thought again of how light she had felt and the stillness of the sky. Someday soon, she decided, she was going to ride in a hot-air balloon again. Perhaps one day she might even become a balloonist herself! It was such a wild idea that she laughed out loud.

As the whirligig wheel lifted her upward, Sophie was smiling. She was dreaming fabulous dreams of flying — of drifting on and on through the clouds into a wide and wonderful blue sky.

About the Real Sophie Blanchard

Sophie Blanchard was born in a village near La Rochelle in France in 1778 and grew up to become one of the world's first female aeronauts.

Not much is known about Sophie's childhood or her family, so for this story I have imagined her mama and an older sister, Flora. Historians think Sophie made her first hot-air balloon ride when she was sixteen, but I have imagined a secret balloon adventure that could have happened when she was even younger!

When she grew up, Sophie married the balloonist Jean-Pierre Blanchard and was soon well known across Europe for the amazing balloon flights she made with her husband. After Jean-Pierre died in 1809, Sophie went on working as a solo balloonist. She became famous for her daring nighttime flights, for launching fireworks from her balloon and for dangerous adventures like crossing the Alps by balloon (where the temperature dropped so low that icicles formed on her hands and face!). She was a favorite of Napoleon and was later made France's "Official Aeronaut" by King Louis XVIII. She

died in 1819 in Paris, after an accident
when her balloon caught fire.

Today, the girl who was once
too afraid to ride in a carriage is
remembered as a bold adventurer and
an important figure in the history of
aviation.

Katherine Woodfine is the author of the stylish and delectable Clockwork Sparrow Mysteries, four wonderful books in which she indulges her love of fashion, adventure and detecting! Katherine lives in London, UK, and is the host of a children's book radio show *Down the Rabbit Hole*. She says that her favorite things are drinking tea and eating cake, wearing red shoes — and writing about the inspirational women of history.

Briony May Smith is a freelance illustrator living in Devon, UK. She grew up in Sandhurst and moved to Cornwall to study illustration at Falmouth University, where she graduated with a 1st Class BA (Hons). She was highly commended for the Macmillan Children's Book Prize in 2013 and 2014, and was shortlisted for the Emerging Talent Category of the British Comic Awards in 2014. Briony takes a lot of inspiration from her rural surroundings.